GW00786499

The Salmon of Knowledge

This story was adapted by author Ann Carroll
and illustrated by Derry Dillon

Published 2019
Poolbeg Press Ltd

123 Grange Hill, Baldoyle
Dublin 13, Ireland

Text © Poolbeg Press Ltd 2013

A catalogue record for this book is available from the British Library.

ISBN 978 1 84223 594 2

All rights reserved. No part of this publication may be reproduced or transmitted in any form or by any means, electronic or mechanical, including photography, recording, or any information storage or retrieval system, without permission in writing from the publisher. The book is sold subject to the condition that it shall not, by way of trade or otherwise, be lent, resold or otherwise circulated without the publisher's prior consent in any form of binding or cover other than that in which it is published and without a similar condition, including this condition, being imposed on the subsequent purchaser.

1

Cover design and illustrations by Derry Dillon
Printed by GPS Colour Graphics Ltd, Alexander Road, Belfast BT6 9HP

The Salmon of Knowledge

Also in the Nutshell series

The Children of Lir
How Cúchulainn Got His Name
The Story of Saint Patrick
The Salmon of Knowledge
The Story of the Giant's Causeway
The Story of Newgrange
Granuaile – The Pirate Queen
Oisín and Tír na nÓg
The Story of Brian Boru
Deirdre of the Sorrows
Heroes of the Red Branch Knights
The Adventures of the Fianna
The Adventures of Maebh – The Warrior Queen
Diarmuid and Gráinne and the Vengeance of Fionn
Saint Brigid the Fearless
The Vikings in Ireland
Journey into the Unknown – The Story of Saint Brendan
The Story of Tara
Niall of the Nine Hostages
The Magical Story of the Tuatha Dé Danann
Saint Colmcille (Also known as Saint Columba)
The Little Book of Irish Saints

When he was a child, Fionn Mac Cumhaill was always asking questions. He wanted to know everything and always listened to the answers. He particularly wanted to know how his father, Cumhall, had died. But it wasn't until his seventh birthday that his mother thought him old enough to understand. And this was the story she told:

"Your father was the leader of the Fianna. They are the bravest and the strongest warriors in Ireland and also the most clever.

To be one of them, a young man has to take on many challenges. Armed only with a stick and a shield he has to stand against nine men while they let fly their spears. He must not allow a weapon to get by him or to hurt him.

Then he has to run silently through the woods. Not a twig can snap or a leaf rustle. Nor can his long hair get caught in a branch or bramble. And he has to be able to jump over obstacles at chest height without slowing down, while staying ahead of the hunters who give him only a small start. And if he gets a thorn in his foot he must be able to pick it out without changing his speed.

He also has to know the twelve books of Bardic poetry, be a poet in his own right and be wise in his opinions.

If he passes all these tests, then and only then can he join the Fianna."

Fionn's mother paused, remembering many things, and Fionn said, "I would like to grow up to be such a warrior."

She nodded. “It’s what your father would have wished. He was the greatest of these warriors and became their leader. He was also the smartest, except when it came to love.

When we met he asked if I would be his wife. But my father, your grandfather, detested Cumhall, as he would have hated any man who loved me. He would not allow the marriage so Cumhall took me away and we were wed."

She stopped and Fionn could see how sad she was and he stayed silent.

Presently she went on. "My father complained to the High King, insisting I'd been kidnapped. Cumhall was outlawed and he was no longer allowed to lead the Fianna. Instead he was seen as an enemy.

The new leader was Goll Mac Morna and your father was killed by him in battle."

"But I thought he was the bravest and the best," Fionn interrupted. "How could he have been beaten?"

"Because he was troubled. To fight the battle he had to leave me and he was worried about my safety. You see, I was expecting you, Fionn, and when my father heard this news he ordered that I be caught and burned to death."

Fionn gasped, "That's horrible."

"And I think Cumhall was distracted with worry on the day of battle and that's how he was defeated."

Fionn took in all his mother told him. Something still puzzled him, though he thought he knew the answer. "Is that why we're always moving from one place to the next? Because your father would kill us both if he found us?"

She shook her head. "No, the High King has ordered him to leave us in peace. But we keep moving because you might be in danger from Goll Mac Morna, who sees you as his enemy and believes you will one day claim leadership of the Fianna."

Fionn drew himself up and said, "I would like to do that, Mother."

She smiled. "Good. It will take time. You must learn a lot before then, but I've found you the best teacher in the world! You'll be safe with him as he's greatly respected."

And so it was that Fionn went to study with Finnegas, a wise man who lived on the banks of the Boyne.

The boy learned much. In time he became an expert hunter and fisherman and was swifter than the hare. He could find the best honey and

the sweetest wild fruit. Learning came easily and he knew all the great poets and created his own fine verse. Best of all, by the time he was in his teens he was a master of spear and sword.

These things the wise man taught him, but one thing he kept back.

All of his life Finnegas had searched for absolute knowledge. He wanted to know everything and realised he fell far short of this goal.

In his quest he learned about the Salmon of Knowledge, a fish who had gained all the wisdom in the world from eating the first hazelnuts that had fallen into the Boyne from a circle of nine magic hazel trees. Now the first person to taste the salmon would gain this knowledge.

For many years Finnegas searched the Boyne and told no one of his quest, not even Fionn.

Then one day at noon while he was resting near a pool on the river, he noticed a number of hazel trees. Idly he counted them.

Nine. In a circle.

Nine. Nine! Nine!

Finnegas jumped up and ran to the bank and when he looked down into the cool water he saw the mighty golden fish, its eyes bright with all the knowledge of the world.

So began his fight to catch the salmon. Every day he tried and failed. Often he thought it was laughing at his efforts. Always the bait was taken but never the hook. Sometimes the fish jumped through the water into the air, did a twirl and bowed before plunging away.

Fionn watched the battle with great interest. He wanted to have a go, but Finnegas refused. After months, Fionn said to him, “I might be luckier. Let me help.” And tired of failure, Finnegas let him try.

Soon the boy got a pull on the end of his line. This had happened before and Finnegas thought nothing of it. Then Fionn said, "Maybe if you help me we can pull him in between us." It was worth a try.

The struggle went on for hours. Often the two were nearly tugged into the water. Their arms ached and their legs felt like jelly, and the fish splashed them till they were soaked. But at last, very slowly, they got the salmon onto the bank where it breathed its last.

"We must cook it immediately! Set the fire, Fionn, and when it's ready we will share this mighty meal, but I must have the first mouthful. Give me your promise not to eat any before me, not a morsel. And don't ask why!"

Fionn promised and though he was curious he didn't ask.

But Finnegas was so tired that he fell asleep beside the fire the boy prepared and Fionn decided to cook the fish for him.

The salmon smelled delicious and Fionn's mouth watered in anticipation, though he was mindful of his promise. Then he saw a blister rising on the salmon from the heat and, afraid the fish might burn, he pressed his thumb against

it to see if it was cooked. When a spurt of hot fat burned his thumb he put it into his mouth at once to ease the pain. The salmon was ready.

He lifted the fish onto a platter and woke his teacher.

Immediately Finnegas saw something different in Fionn. “You have tasted the salmon!” he said. “Your eyes are bright with the world’s knowledge. How could you betray me?”

“I haven’t tasted it. Yours will be the first mouthful as we agreed.”

Finnegas knew the boy always kept his word but he could see the change in him.

"Tell me what happened as you were cooking it." And when the boy told him how he had put his burnt thumb into his mouth, Finnegas realised at once that he'd missed his only chance and told Fionn, "You've had first taste of the Salmon of Knowledge, though you did not mean to. Now you will be the wisest poet, the best warrior and the greatest leader.

To know the answer to any question all you have to do is bite the thumb you burned. I can teach you no more."

And so they parted and Fionn went on his way.

He sought out the Fianna at Royal Tara without saying who he was. The warriors thought him far too young to join their ranks but he proved himself by passing all the tests with ease. They were greatly impressed and made him one of their own. Then Fionn decided to show he was the best of all the warriors by taking on another challenge.

Every year at Samhain the fire-breathing spirit Aillen sent the Fianna to sleep and burned Tara to the ground. The warriors were at their wits' end, knowing they would fail to stay awake and it would happen again.

But this year Fionn fought off sleep. He did so by piercing his forehead with his spear whenever he felt drowsy. When Aillen breathed ferocious flames, Fionn's great cloak was ready to put them out and before the fire-breather could recover from the shock he killed him with the spear.

When the Fianna awoke, they were most grateful, for Fionn had given them back their pride. Learning who he was, Goll Mac Morna no longer saw him as an enemy, but accepted him as leader, and afterwards was proud to fight by his side.

Fionn became the greatest chieftain the Fianna ever had. Stories of his great deeds were retold through the centuries. There are those who say he is not dead but sleeping in a deep cavern beneath the sea, surrounded

by his warriors and that one day when Ireland needs him, he will wake to the sound of the horn and be a hero once again.

The End

If you enjoyed this book from Poolbeg why not visit our website

WWW.POOLBEG.COM

and get another book delivered straight to your home or to a friend's home.

All books despatched within 24 hours.

FREE POSTAGE on orders over €10 in Rep. of Ireland*

Why not join our mailing list at www.poolbeg.com and get some fantastic offers, competitions, author interviews, new releases and much more?

POOLBEG ON SOCIAL MEDIA

@PoolbegBooks

poolbegbooks

www.facebook.com/poolbegpress

*Free postage in Ireland on orders over €10 and Europe on orders over €65.